Clauaia
The Caterpillar™

Andrew McDonough

Claudia the caterpillar lived in the garden. She spent her days crawling on the plants and eating the flowers.

One day Claudia saw butterflies flying and gliding, winging and wheeling across the sky.

"Now, that's the life for me!" said Claudia.

So Claudia climbed up the big old tree.

She stood on the highest branch.

"It's the butterfly life for me," said Claudia.

"I'm going to
FLYYYYYYYyyyyyyyyyyyyyy.............."
Thud.

Next day Claudia watched the butterflies flying and gliding, winging and wheeling across the sky. "Yes, that's the life for me," she said. "I would love to be flying and gliding, winging . . . wings! I need wings!"

So Claudia made some wings. She climbed to the top of the big old tree, stretched out her wings and yelled, "It's the butterfly life for me. I'm going to FLYYYYYYYYyyyyyyyyyyyyyy…………."

Thud.

Next day Claudia watched the butterflies flying and gliding, winging and wheeling across the sky. She decided to ask God about what she wanted. "God, I want to fly like the butterflies."

So God led Claudia up the big old tree and under the highest branch. He attached her to the branch and began forming a chrysalis around her like a shell. "Hey," cried Claudia, "I want to fly. If you close me up in here I'll die!"

But God kept covering Claudia until she was completely closed up in the chrysalis.

Claudia stayed in the chrysalis all day and all night and all the next day. One week, two weeks, three weeks, wrapped up in the chrysalis.

Then the chrysalis shook. Rip. Out popped Claudia — good old Claudia, wonderful new Claudia.

She flexed and flapped . . . and flew.

"This is the life," cried Claudia as she went flying and gliding, winging and wheeling across the sky.

The Back Page

Claudia the Caterpillar comes from Jesus' promise in John 10:10 and the promise about Jesus in 2 Corinthians 5:17.

You can use this story to grow children's awareness that life, in all its fullness, comes through Jesus.

Before the story

Begin by saying:
"Let me tell you about one of God's friends who wanted to enjoy life to the full."

Read the story

After the story

Ask, "What did it take for Claudia to fly?" and let your conversation grow from there.

God's blessing,

Andrew